For Aunty Ann and Uncle Roy.
Thank you for always supporting
everything I do on my creative journey.
Lots of love xxx
—L.E.A.

Philomel Books
An imprint of Penguin Random House LLC, New York

First published in the United States of America by Philomel,
an imprint of Penguin Random House LLC, 2020.

First published in Great Britain by Bloomsbury Publishing Plc in 2020.

Visit us online at penguinrandomhouse.com

Library of Congress Cataloging-in-Publication Data is available.

Manufactured in China.

ISBN 9780593117286

1 3 5 7 9 10 8 6 4 2

Edited by Liza Kaplan. • Design by Ellice Lee.
Text set in Typography of Coop.

LAURA ELLEN ANDERSON

I DON'T WANT TO BE QUIET!

PHILOMEL BOOKS

NOOOOO

OOOOOOOO!

I don't want
to be quiet,

I'd rather be

LOUD!

I want to be HEARD and
stand out from the crowd!

It's SO MUCH more fun,
when you're NOISY like ME...
I don't understand
why Mom doesn't agree.

Mom whispers,
"Be quiet. Your brother
is sleeping."

But, OOPS, it's too late,
now the baby is weeping.

At school I love

CHATTING

and

LAUGHING

and

CLAPPING,

but my teacher gets angry and then ends up snapping.

"ENOUGH!
Please be quiet!
You must listen in school."

But silence in class is a terrible rule!

Stairs are
for STOMPING,

THUMP!

spoons are
for DRUMMING,

and when my mom's working,
I help her by HUMMING.

Tin cans are for CLANGING,

balloons are for POPPING.

Mom REALLY hates that...

but I AM NOT STOPPING.

Food is for CRUNCHING

and drinks are for SLURPING.

QUIET PLEASE.

My feet are for SPLASHING,

my mouth is for BURPING (oops)! BUT...

So I make silly noises and shuffle my chair.
I twiddle my thumbs and fiddle my hair.

I huff and I puff and I finally BURST...

"SHHHHH! We're reading.
Talk quietly please!"

I stop ... And I frown ...
Then I stare at my knees.

My cheeks go all red, so I pick up a book—
maybe I'll give this a really quick look . . .

Page after page
I'm completely SPELLBOUND.

HOURS have passed, and
I've not made a SOUND.

But INSIDE my head there's a whole lot of NOISE—
magical quests—pirate girls and lost boys!

Next morning I LISTEN, and what do I hear?
Birds tweeting and singing their new morning cheer.

And then while at school,
I learn lots of new things

about **numbers**

and **poems**

and the reigns of **great kings.**

I like being quiet.
It means I **HEAR MORE**
of the small gentle sounds
that I couldn't before . . .

But there are still LOTS of places and times to be LOUD...

When I'm
DRUMMING
and

DANCING
and...

TAP

TAP

making Mom proud!